Which NOSE for WITCH?

Written by
David Crosby

Illustrated by
Carolina Coroa

Grizelda is a baby witch,
She's such a pretty sight.
Her dainty little button nose
Won't give the world a **FRIGHT**.

But now Grizelda's growing up
A special day has come.
She's off to choose her grown-up nose,
A super **WITCHY** one!

She steps into 'The Conk Boutique'
And can't believe her eyes!
Rows of noses fill the shelves,
There's every **SHAPE** and **SIZE**!

This book belongs to:

_____

_____

_____

Which Nose for Witch?

An original concept by author David Crosby

© David Crosby

Illustrated by Carolina Coroa

MAVERICK ARTS PUBLISHING LTD
Studio 11, City Business Centre, 6 Brighton Road, Horsham,
West Sussex, RH13 5BB, +44 (0)1403 256941
© Maverick Arts Publishing Limited 2021
Published September 2021

A CIP catalogue record for this book
is available at the British Library.

ISBN 978-1-84886-760-4

www.maverickbooks.co.uk

With thanks and
love to my family
- D.C.

For Samy and Teresa
- C.C.

"Now don't be shy!" her mother cries,
"Just pick a nose that's ace.
Then I shall cast my **NOSE-SWAP** spell
To try it on your face!"

Grizelda picks a pointy one,
With two **WARTS** on the end.

Her mother waves her magic wand –

Griz feels her nose extend!

"Oh Griz," says Mum, "you're gorgeous girl!
Like something from a dream!"
"This nose is not ideal..." says Griz,

"...When eating an **ICE CREAM!**"

Grizelda picks a hook-shaped nose,
It's **BUMPY** and it's **SCARY**.

Her mother waves her magic wand –
Griz feels her nose grow **HAIRY**!

"Oh Griz," says Mum, "it's beautiful!
You look **COMPLETELY** witchy!"

"This nose feels really bad," says Griz.
"It's **TINGLY** and it's **ITCHY**!"

As Griz turns down each frightful nose
A crowd appears, wide-eyed.

Mum takes her daughter by the hand,
And marches her outside.

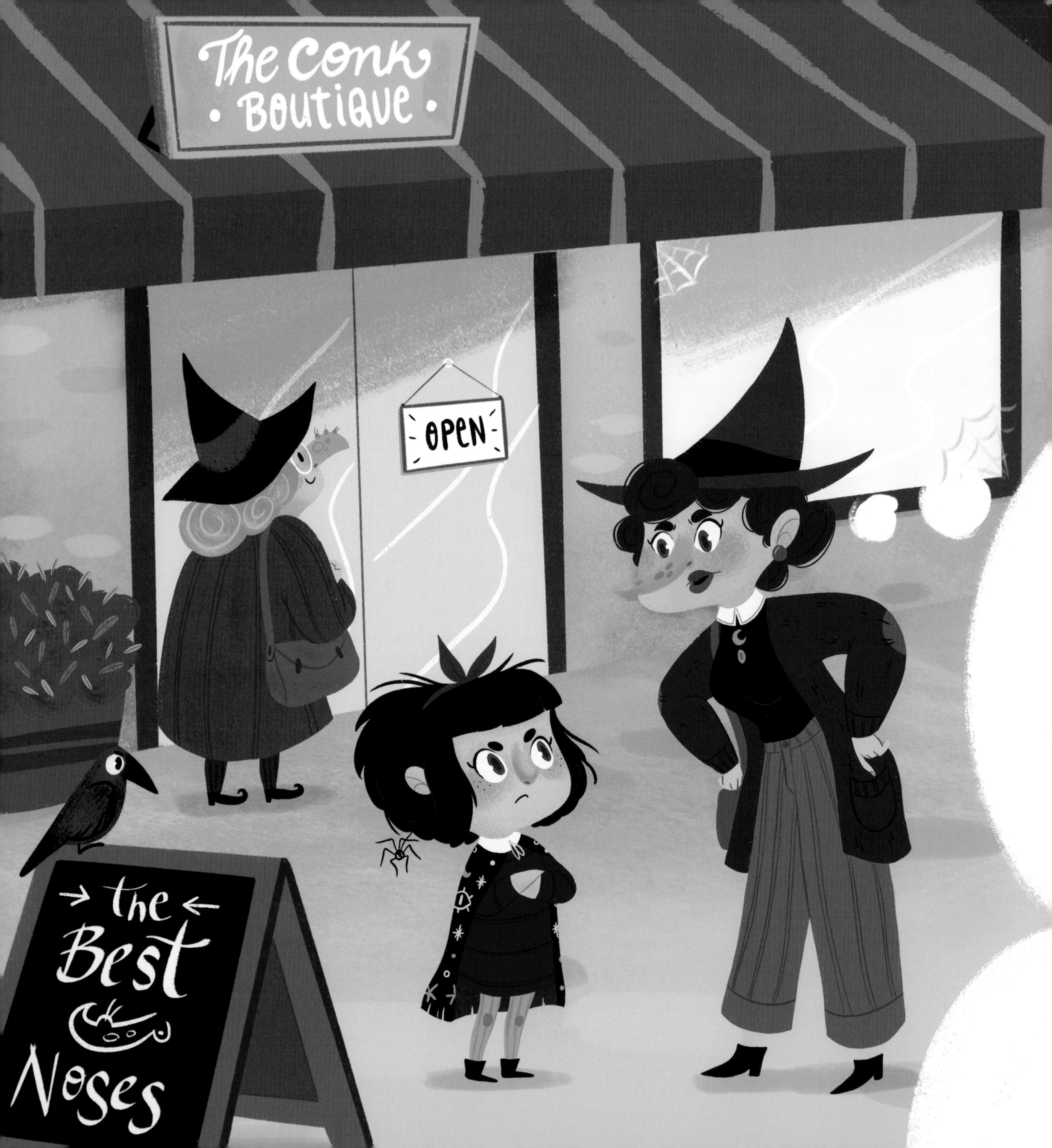
The Conk Boutique
OPEN
the Best Noses

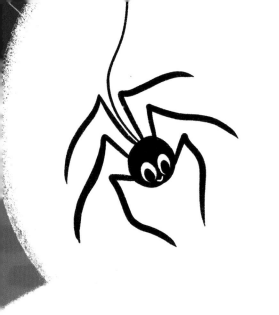

"Now Griz," says Mum, "**ENOUGH** of this!
I won't stand one more hitch!
You've **GOT** to choose a grown-up nose
To be a grown-up witch!"

"Says who?" says Griz and turns away
Pretending not to care.

Then something shimmers in the light
And Griz can only stare.

"I've seen the nose I want," says Griz.
"My witch life starts **TODAY**!"
"At last!" says Mum, "Which nose is it?
I'll buy it right away!"

"Well," says Griz, "this nose won't ITCH
And ice cream will be fine.
Come here and have a look at it,
The nose I LOVE is...

...MINE!"

"But **NO** witch keeps her baby nose,
Oh Griz, this is the **WORST**."

"Hmmm," says Griz, "no witch you say?
Then I shall be the FIRST!"

So while most witches change their nose,
In search of witch perfection,

Griz feels grown-up and confident,
And **LOVES** her own reflection!

Mmm... YUM!